THE KING OF DAMS

by

Susan Trott

Susan Trott

Copyright

Copyright © 2025, Susan Trott

ISBN-13: 978-1-998107-52-0

First Edition, November 2025
Printed in the United States by IngramSpark

Table of Contents

Susan Trott

I. Triumph

They named it in ten languages and none of them were humble. The King of Dams. The Crown. The Great Stillness. On the morning the gates closed and the river became a polished blade, flags trembled along the parapet and the air smelled of wet stone and diesel and new paint. The water, held back for the first time in its life, took a slow breath against the wall and exhaled mist into the sun. Helicopters circled. Brass bands tuned, audibly nervous at the scale of the canyon and the acoustics of a gorge that had learned to swallow sound.

Dignitaries stood in a line like rivets. Their smiles had the bright varnish of money and sleep deprivation. They wore lapel pins in the shape of a stylized wave, a lightning bolt trapped inside it. Cameras clung to scaffolds and rails. Drone swarms hummed into geometric patience. This was the day humanity would put its thumb on the scale and the planet would nod along, cooperative at last.

The Engineer stood back from the stage and touched the concrete as if taking a pulse. She had been here long before the speeches: through the nights of cold joints and admixtures, the days of tilted sun and vibrating trucks, the months when wind laid grit into every lunch. She knew the wall's secret geometry—the stone's weight and the river's ambition, the way the foundation keyed into bedrock that had never been asked to hold such silence. She could still recite the final pour schedule from memory. She had loved numbers as a child, but this was different: an affection for something that could crush her without noticing. When the MC said her name for the crowd to cheer, she smiled and lifted a hand; her palm left a gray print on her suit.

Down on the drowned margin, where a road had once braided through orchards and a schoolhouse had kept a blue door, the Villager watched from the prow of a state boat. The deck was pricked with confetti from a ribbon-cutting earlier upriver. Officials had invited "representatives of resettled communities," a phrase he heard in three syllables: re-set-tled, like a chair scraped back and made to fit somewhere else. His grandmother had been buried on a hillside that would tonight be a brown shadow beneath ten meters of green water. When the dam was rumored, he'd taken a tape measure to the church and found the height of the eaves, then stood on the ridge with a survey map and held the tape in the wind until it snapped. This morning the reservoir licked the new shoreline with a cat's deliberate tongue. On deck, he rubbed the river's grit between finger and thumb and wondered if remembering counted as resistance or only as salt.

Far from the crowd and the choreography, in a trailer that smelled of plastic and coffee, the Scientist watched the screens where satellites turned raw light into numbers.

                    Susan Trott

Her team had worked a miracle of their own—borrowing time from instruments that had been meant to map glaciers and the jitter of tectonic plates. The curves she traced were tiny, honest things. Micro-variations in gravity. The postural sway of the crust under burden. The sort of data that made people clear their throats on television and say words like negligible and within expectations. She did not disagree. She simply understood that negligible, repeated enough times over enough area, learns to pronounce itself.

Outside, the speeches began. The first minister said the dam would "secure the century." The energy secretary called it "a battery the size of a sea." The international consortium's chair compared it to the Moon landing, then corrected himself with a laugh—"No, the Moon landing compared to this"—and the crowd was happy to let the joke stand. Someone read a poem that had taken no risks. A ten-year-old from the nearest new town pressed a chrome button that did exactly nothing; somewhere out of sight, a control room enacted the ceremony's cause.

The wall itself did not care. It accepted the new pressure with the same indifference it would one day offer the old. Men had argued over arch vs. gravity vs. buttress; the river had voted for whatever didn't move. The Engineer, listening to the speeches, recounted load paths the way some people pray. She could feel the heat still living in the concrete—metabolic, like an animal digesting a long meal. When she closed her eyes, she could imagine the reservoir that would be: a bruise of blue pushed into the folds of the basin, then a sheet, then a continent of contained weather. She could nearly hear it, the low massed murmur of a new inland sea practicing its vowels.

"We ask the Earth to partner with us," the second minister said, which was one way to name it. A choir sang. Two hawks used the updrafts like stairs and refused to look impressed.

On the boat, the Villager's neighbor pointed out landmarks like a grieving tour guide. There, the almond grove that had been replanted twice after late frosts; there, the mark on the cliff where the flood of '72 had peaked; there, the snake rock where children took dares and a boy had split his head open like a melon, and somehow the memory made everyone laugh even now. The Villager nodded and kept his own cartography: the rhythm of wheels on a bridge that no longer existed, the summer stink of fish guts and mint near the cannery, the taste of iron that a thunderstorm put on your tongue. The loudspeakers on the dam threw the minister's voice out across the reach, warped by wind and echoes into something ancient and unintelligible. He found himself liking it that way.

The Scientist's phone vibrated with a message from an analyst in the city: *Congrats on your big day. Try not to look too serious on camera.* She smiled and typed back a picture of the curve she was watching—minute deflection plotted over hours, a graceful line that stole a millimeter here and loaned it there, and then she deleted the unsent message

                    Susan Trott

because people read tone into graphs, and she was not in the mood to be told to relax. She loved the planet because it was complicated and did not need her love in return. From the trailer's doorway she could see the water darken as it deepened, a color shift like a bruise blooming. The first breeze off the new surface had a taste of copper and clay, and behind it she could almost sense a second wind, colder and higher, coming from a place maps did not yet draw.

The ribbon was enormous—red as a warning and wide as a road. Handsome men in hardhats handed golden scissors to people who did not know how to hold them. The cut, when it came, made a ragged sound that microphones had not planned for. Confetti cannons fired. The drones translated into a word that hung in the air in block letters: TOGETHER. The crowd cheered; the drones rearranged themselves into a number—the projected gigawatts—and the cheers became an applause with the confidence of arithmetic behind it.

The Engineer was ushered to the microphone. She had rehearsed gratitude. She thanked crews by name, concrete plants, the teams who had mapped the paleontology in the cliffs and moved fossils gently as eggs. She thanked weather, for mostly behaving. She thanked the river itself, and there the crowd softened; it was always good when someone spoke as if the river were a person. She did not say what else she wanted to thank: accident, luck, the stubbornness of rock, her own fear that had made her double-check the cold joint at Pier 17 the night the wind came hard and sideways. She did not say, because the moment did not have room for it, that success at this size felt less like victory than like postponement.

On the water, the boat's engine coughed and settled. A flock of gulls rose, arguing, and dropped again to peck at whatever the rising reservoir had offered them from the newly drowned: insects, seeds, the small disordered lives that shuffled when mammoth things moved. The Villager watched the new shoreline where cottonwoods had once kept the river honest. Now their tops were leafing under water, pale fists undone into green.

Reporters leaned microphones toward the Scientist and asked questions with question marks that had already made up their minds. *Is it safe?* Yes. *Will the lake change the weather?* Locally, in ways we can model. *Is it true some of your colleagues expect to detect rotational changes?* The Earth is exquisitely sensitive; we will observe tiny effects, yes. *Tiny.* Tiny. The word became a charm she offered strangers and, to her surprise, herself. When they had gone, she traced a fingertip across the edge of her screen and felt the fatigue inside her wrists like someone else's heartbeat.

Near noon, the sun stood without apology and the concrete warmed to a skin-temperature that made the Engineer swallow against the sense that the wall was alive. The turbines purred like polite animals learning house rules. Beyond the spillway, the river performed its

Susan Trott

new trick: a deliberate restraint, a script, a choreography of flow. It looked orderly. It sounded almost content.

There are moments when history is awed by its own costume. As the dignitaries collected themselves for photographs—backs straight, chins lifted, smiles pre-installed—the King of Dams let a deep vibration pass through itself the way a man lets a thought go by. No one felt it on the platform. On the boat, the Villager put a palm to the rail and did not register anything beyond the beat of his own blood. In the trailer, the Scientist's curve flickered a pixel and returned to its trend line with docile obedience. The hawks wrote lazy S's on the updraft and found, for a second, a column of air that did not behave, then let it go.

The band struck a march that had been practiced under fluorescent light and now sounded brave. Children in white shirts waved. The crowd's noise rose and fell like a breathing creature and then arranged itself into a sustained cheer, the kind people produce when they want to hear themselves part of a success. It was, in fairness, a success. An improbable, back-breaking, ledger-spanning, world-tilting success. The Engineer allowed herself that word for one heartbeat and then, exactly as she had trained herself to do, she turned and looked not at the wall but at the valley, the basin, the sky. She did not know what she was looking for. She would later tell herself, with a scientist's superstition, that she had been listening.

By late afternoon the light leaned gold and forgiving. The reservoir's face mirrored a single cloud into an elongated myth. Photographers found angles that made the dam look eternal. Politicians practiced their legacy sentences under their breath. Tour buses arranged themselves into checkered patience. Someone started a chant; someone else started another, and the two chanted together for a while until they learned how to alternate. The day's heat lifted into a higher, paler heat, the kind that turns distance into a shimmer.

At the edge of the new waterline, a child in a yellow shirt threw a stone and waited to hear it splash. The stone never spoke. It slid into a silence large enough to hold it without complaint. The child threw another, then another, then turned to ask his mother why the lake swallowed so quietly. She opened her mouth to answer and found she did not have a word ready, so she kissed his hair and said, "Listen. It's learning to be still."

On the platform the last ribbon's last thread let go, a red filament lifted by a thermal to dance, to loop, to be admired by a hawk and missed by a camera. The wall at their backs was a cliff humans had convinced themselves belonged to them, and for the length of a ceremony it did. A breeze came off the newborn sea carrying the cool promise of evening and a smell like rain that had never fallen. People sighed without knowing why. They had made a lake. They had made a future. They had taught a river to hold its breath.

     Susan Trott

Far below their pride and promises, in a darkness older than any speech, the first molecules of water touched a seam of hot rock and changed state without permission.

Susan Trott

II. SETTLING AND SIGNS

By the second week the valley had a new sound. It wasn't the turbines or the march of trucks hauling landscaping to the visitor center. It was quieter than that—a long vowel in the throat of the basin, a pressure-word. In town, doors that had always shut flush now kissed their jambs and stuck. A woman who ran the bakery propped hers with a bag of flour and called it charming; by afternoon she had planed the door and found the planing did not help. Floors learned a slope you could feel only when a marble wandered. Pictures leaned south on their nails. A carpenter tried to blame humidity, then remembered he'd said the same thing in winter.

The Engineer walked the crest before dawn, when the concrete held night's cool and the reservoir wore a skin of mist that peeled away in languid strips. She checked the readouts embedded in the parapet like braille: strain gauges, thermistors, tiltmeters with their patient decimals. On her tablet a diagram of the dam glowed with tiny, obedient greens. Everything was within expectations. A drone returned from an automatic shoreline survey and settled on its pad with a sound like a sigh. She placed a palm to the parapet out of habit and felt a sensation she could not name—neither vibration nor stillness, but a memory of both.

Upriver, where the new shore had converted orchards into drowned ghosts, the Villager pulled up the slatted lid of his well and dipped a tin cup. The water came up the color of brewed tea. He swirled it, watched silt spiral like a thought, poured it onto the dry lawn. His granddaughter, whose legs had never known the old riverbank as a daily friend, asked if the lake tasted different than the river. He told her yes, but he could not explain how. That night when he lay on the mattress he felt something through the springs: not shaking, exactly. A heavy animal turning in sleep far beneath the house.

The Scientist had persuaded her boss to let her keep the trailer by the dam for one month past ceremony. She slept there on a narrow cot because leaving felt like breaking a conversation in the middle. The satellite curves still drew their tiny lies—noise and truth married in inconvenient intimacy. She watched the gravity field adjust to the reservoir's weight like a taut skin pushed by a fingertip. She watched the crust's minute deflection trace a curve with the grace of a dancer who knew precisely how far to bend and no further. She'd always liked the way Earth absorbed insults—ice sheets, tides, heat—and converted them to motion measured in millimeters. The kindness of it made her uneasy now.

In the city, the papers ran photo essays of sunbathers on new beaches, fishermen grinning with unfamiliar species that had wandered in from somewhere and decided to stay. "Lake Culture Blooms," one headline said, and the photos did not lie: children discovered a thousand ways to

     Susan Trott

throw stones, teenagers found corners for privacy, old men relearned the names of winds. The dam's electrics did what they had promised; lights steadied in neighborhoods that had been accustomed to the flicker of indecision. People said together a lot. They meant it.

Beneath the dam—behind the glamour, in galleries that wore sweat like weather—the Engineer's crew checked foundation drains. Steel pipes hissed with seepage caught and tamed. She ran her hands along condensate-slick walls and read the pulse in the drip. "We're good," her deputy said, and they were. Good didn't stop her from dreaming of the night months ago when she had woken certain she'd forgotten to pin a cold joint. In the dream she tore the dam apart with her fingernails to see. In the morning she'd laughed because that was not how concrete worked, and then she hadn't laughed because sometimes fear did.

The first tremor barely roused dogs. A low clink of plates, a ripple through railings, a report from a geophone in a pasture that the Scientist would have missed if she hadn't been awake for no reason. She marked it on her map with a dot the size of a freckle and went back to the long, quiet slope of things. The second tremor made a stack of cheap saucers in the bakery shift their loyalties. The owner swore in a way she apologized for to no one. In a farmhouse thirty miles away a man sitting to lace his boots felt the floor move and told himself he'd stood too quickly.

Within expectations, the structural health report said. Within expectations, the Energy Secretary repeated in his afternoon briefing, even though no one had asked. The phrase began to feel like a coat everyone was expected to wear into every weather.

At the water's edge, where cottonwood trunks had become monument shafts to a forgotten sky, the Villager noticed a new ooze between roots: fine bubbles purled up with a sound too small to belong to the world as he knew it. He crouched and watched the little glints break the surface, silver and unhurried. He put a finger into the silt and felt warmth. He stared at his finger as if it had misinformed him. When he told his neighbor, she said the lake makes its own weather, and he nodded because that sounded wise enough to keep for later.

The Scientist arranged her dots—tremor positions—across a map that had not been printed yet by anyone who mattered. Her graduate student, looping in by video, observed that the pattern looked like a windshield struck by a rock, except the impact point was an absence rather than a presence. The Scientist, who had grown up on a river that made its own rules each spring, said nothing. She remembered the day she'd learned the difference between brittle and ductile and how the words were everything and nothing like their metaphorical lives. Rocks, burdened, could forget they were meant to be rock.

                          Susan Trott

At a town hall put together by the power company, a man with a neat beard and compassionate eyebrows explained that microseismicity was a normal response to load and pore-pressure changes. He said reservoir-induced seismicity as if it tasted of reassurance. An older woman asked if her gravestones would move. He said they would not. The Villager asked if the floor of his cousin's barn would continue to slope until the cows walked like sailors. The man with the eyebrows smiled and said cows adapted better than humans in most circumstances. People laughed because they wanted one another to.

The week grew hot. The reservoir sent up a breath at noon that carried a new taste—mineral and green, unfamiliar as a stranger's aftershave. The Engineer watched the mist that had been content to lie in early morning begin to lift earlier, linger later, coarsen. Vortices formed at points along the shore and wandered inland like visitors who had not been invited and did not think an invitation was required. She put a hand on the parapet and felt, unmistakably this time, a note passing through the wall—low, long, almost amused. She could not tell if it came from water or rock.

On a Thursday, the first true quake introduced itself like a handshake from someone who didn't know their own strength. Crockery marched toward edges. Drawers rattled. A gas station canopy shivered and spoke a syllable with its rivets. The dam took the motion as a body takes a cough. Traffic slowed on the crest. The Engineer's phone did what phones do in emergencies: decided to be both too helpful and not helpful at all. In the trailer the Scientist watched her dots connect themselves into thin ribs and spines, a silent anatomy assembling. She clicked a tool to compute a centroid and got back a location that was everywhere and nowhere—the kind of answer that makes people turn their palms up and ask to see the math.

A video went minor-viral: a glass of water on a kitchen table, surface trembling with concentric rings that looked staged until a spoon slid across the table without a hand to help it. Someone laid the theme from an old movie under the clip. Someone else subtitled the rings with the names of politicians. Humor found its old rut in new weather.

"Settlement," the project website said, "is normal in large geo-structures," and posted two graphs rendered in a reassuring palette. The Villager's granddaughter drew a picture of the lake for school and put a big happy face in the water. Her teacher taped it to a bulletin board beside a poster of cloud types which, lately, had been teaching the children very little.

The Engineer requested additional piezometers along the left abutment. She used a sentence she knew would make procurement move: conservative, out of an abundance, and the word monitoring, which was nobody's enemy. Her deputy asked if she was worried. She said she did not believe in worry, only in measurements, and the deputy allowed himself the kindness of believing her. In the night she dreamed she was kneeling on the riverbed, pressing

     Susan Trott

her ear to gravel to listen for something that either was or was not there.

"Negligible," the politician said again in a morning show interview, the way you say abracadabra. The host nodded with the practiced empathy of a man who had not spent a night listening to his house negotiate with its foundation. The Scientist clicked through to the stream, muted it, unmuted it, muted it again. She wrote an email to a colleague in another country and deleted the adjective she had used for the pattern on her map, because adjectives were promises and she was not ready to make one.

In the fields below the dam, men staked new grape rows in soil that trembled by rumor alone. A boy on a bicycle rolled down a street that had learned a new slope and crashed where there had never been a curb. The villager's neighbor's grandson texted: *Did u feel that???* and he wrote back, *It is the earth adjusting to compliments.*

By month's end the instruments had the long look of systems that have decided not to be boring. The gravity anomaly that had seemed as innocent as a blanket now tucked itself with intent. The tiltmeters, steady as saints, learned to nod. The Engineer took the stairs down to the galleries more often. In the lower air her hair frizzed, and her breath found a rhythm that matched the drip.

"Your dots," the graduate student said on a Saturday, "are running ahead of the predictions," and the Scientist resisted the urge to field-upgrade the word predictions to warnings. Her models wanted a center they could not find. The tremors were not behaving as a chorus around a stage. They were rehearsing for something where there was no stage yet.

At the newly minted marina, tourists tied their white boats to bright cleats and listened to the weather on their phones. The app said breezy. The lake, at late afternoon, began to throw thin streamers into the sky—steam wisps that braided and unbraided again like the hair of someone thinking. The Villager stood with his granddaughter and watched a coil of vapor walk itself shoreward and lay a skin of damp over the road. When he touched the hood of his truck an hour later, it had beaded with water as if rain had visited and forgotten to leave footprints.

———

Susan Trott

III. FRACTURES

The first visible crack appeared where nobody of consequence would see it: in a concrete sidewalk poured in a hurry outside a bait shop that had reinvented itself as a lakeside boutique. It wandered from the edge like a lazy vein, paused at a pebble that should have been screened out, leaped the pebble with a shrug, and continued into a geometry it did not plan to explain. The owner knelt with a stick of chalk and traced it because tracing turned fear into a picture. A woman from the city said it gave the place character.

On the hill behind the visitor center, the lawn that had been unrolled like a rug developed a seam. The seam widened in the heat, narrowed after dark, and learned the mischief of persistence. A groundskeeper drove his mower parallel to it and did not count the ways he could break an axle.

In the slabs of the spillway apron hairlines the color of old milk drew themselves into existence and went patient. The Engineer crouched, ran a fingernail along one, felt it catch. She measured. She wrote the numbers in a notebook because notebooks had weight and Do Not Disturb could not interrupt them. The hairlines did not frighten her; they were part of the great compromise between brain and stone. What bothered her was the noise she could not unhear now when she laid her palm to the dam: a whisper of something larger than hairlines coming true somewhere out of reach.

In the neighborhoods perched on terraces above the lake, people began to keep lists. Things that stuck. Things that hummed. Things that tilted. A woman in a blue house put a marble on her mantle and watched it begin to travel in the afternoon and rest in the morning. She sent a video to the news and the news asked if she had put a wedge under the mantle to make the marble perform. She had not. The news ran the clip with a glib lower third and everyone went back to weather.

The Scientist's map needed larger paper. The dots had discovered each other and were, by increments, agreeing on directions. The pattern—windshield, ice on a winter lake when a stone chooses a place to introduce itself—became explicit. The lines did not converge on the dam. They converged on a basin under the basin, the larger bowl that bedded the smaller. "This isn't load redistribution," she told her boss, and heard herself overstate in a way she had taught students not to. He asked her to write a preliminary note couched in may be and could indicate. She wrote it. She deleted it. She wrote it again, replaced may with the weaker might, hit send, stared at the empty sent box as if it could absolve her.

By then the quakes had developed personalities. There were the low purrs that rounded the edges of your

    Susan Trott

furniture and made the dog lift its head without barking. There were sharp raps that rattled windows like a salesman. And there were long, slow flexures that arrived like weather, walked through every room, and left with a politeness you only appreciated after they were gone. The Villager stood in his yard during one of those and felt the ground pass under him like a tide. He opened his mouth to say something to no one and shut it because there was no phrase sufficient for what his bones had just experienced.

At a regional conference, a geologist put a slide on a screen showing the fault maps before and after. He talked about stress fields and pore pressure and effective normal stress and did not once say the word hubris because science prefers nouns it can put numbers on. In the back row, a team lead from the power company filmed the talk on his phone and sent it to the Energy Secretary's chief of staff, who did not watch it but replied with a thumbs-up.

A farmer in the flatter land downwind sent a letter to the editor about his corn lodging mysteriously—stalks bending at the base and staying down no matter what he did. He blamed seed genetics, weather, God, and then crossed out God because he had been taught you did not write God in the paper for fear of inviting argument. The editorial ran beside a photograph of smiling families on jet skis.

One afternoon, the Engineer and the Scientist met at the parapet without meaning to. They leaned and looked outward as if there were something to see other than the lake practicing how to be forever. "Do you feel it?" the Engineer said, and the question was both too vague and exactly right. The Scientist said, "My maps are inventing a center that isn't where we built one." The Engineer nodded and put her palm to the warm concrete and did not speak the word she had been not speaking for days: rift.

That night the quake that shouldn't have happened did. It did not declare an epicenter the way quakes behave for cameras. It arrived as a persuasion that stretched from one horizon to the other, a long tug that found something in cupboards you thought were safe and invited it to walk. Birds left trees silently. In a hospital, a tray of surgical instruments slid six inches and the surgeon's hand compensated without thinking and then shook afterward when he had time to realize. The dam rode it the way a large animal rides a fly: with the insulted patience of mass.

Morning brought picture-window cracks you could feed a coin into. A ridge-line a county away developed a new shadow, and hikers returning to a trailhead swore they had not walked past that gash the afternoon before. In the gallery beneath the dam, the drip rate on three drains accelerated, then steadied, then lied. The Engineer's deputy said the numbers were still green. The Engineer pressed a hand to the gallery wall and felt what she would later describe to no one as a kindness withdrawing.

When the quake maps came in, the Scientist paced them like a shepherd and found, to her dread and perverse

    Susan Trott

satisfaction, that her windshield had finally met its thrown stone. The lines spidered toward a dark, empty place that, until now, had been assumed to be simply dense. She printed the map and taped it to the wall and stood back and felt the human need to name something you cannot influence. In another life she would have chosen a saint and a candle. In this one she took a felt pen and drew a circle around nothing.

By evening the lake had dressed itself in a new thing: in eddies that idled above places where there had been no wind and no current; in streamers of vapor that braided into rope and unbraided into lace; in a breath that came off the water as if from a creature thinking. People at the marina took pictures and called it beautiful. The Villager sat at the edge of his yard and rubbed dirt between finger and thumb and decided, without flinching from the decision, that beauty at this scale could be a warning in its Sunday clothes.

Clouds learned to form wrong. A long band stood motionless across the horizon while the wind below it tore hedges ragged. In town, the bakery hung a sign that said CLOSED MONDAYS & WHENEVER THE GROUND FEELS FUNNY and sold out of bread before noon. The Engineer ate hers in the truck and read the text from procurement that the extra piezometers would arrive end of week if shipping cooperated. She laughed once sharply in the cab, then hid the laugh in a cough because there was no one to think her unhinged but herself.

That night, the lake talked to the sky. Steam rose and held together, not mist but columns, thin at first, then better at being themselves. They took the moonlight and did new things with it. At two in the morning the Scientist went out of the trailer and lay on the warmth of the dam like someone who has given up important dignity and been delighted by what remains. She listened, because it was all she had that did not require funding, and she heard—not through concrete, not through air, but in her own bones—the long note that had been with them since the ceremony grow one overtone richer.

In the morning the Villager put a stick in the lake and marked its wetness with a pocketknife. He came back after lunch and the water had allowed the stick less to say. He marked it again. In the evening he marked it again. He did not tell anyone. He did not want to share it until he knew whether it was faithlessness in a measuring stick or in what the lake considered itself to be.

The next day, when he came with the stick, he brought his granddaughter and held her head beside the marks. "This much," he said, showing her the day's loss in a gesture even a child could own. She said the lake must be thirsty. He said he thought it was something else. He showed her where the bubbles purled between drowned roots and let her touch the warmth, and when she pulled her finger back, eyes wide, he did not say what he had been thinking

                    Susan Trott

since the first chalk line appeared on the bait-shop walk: that the dam had asked the world to hold its breath, and the world had been polite for longer than anyone had a right to expect.

Susan Trott

IV. Weather of a New Kind

The summer learned a new alphabet. It started with a letter shaped like a haze that never lifted, a soft hand laid on the valley at dawn that refused to be removed by noon. Forecasts said clear and delivered a ceiling of pale milk. The reservoir warmed and began to exhale in sentences; by midafternoon the air tasted like a wet coin and the skin on your wrist gleamed as if remembering rain you had not felt.

Clouds formed wrong. Instead of marching in from the ocean like shipwrecked fleets, they bubbled up over the lake in towers that forgot how to stop. The towers bent downwind into cream-colored anvils that flattened into lids over towns. People learned the new words by damage: downburst, microburst, gust front. A brown river ran down a street that had never practiced being a river. The local news asked an anchor to stand in sideways rain with a microphone whose logo peeled off; the camera showed water falling in sheets so heavy it looked like the air had turned to glass.

Then the lake invented storms that should not have existed inland. Spiral bands coiled lazily for hours, tightening, the wind ordering itself into organization, as if a hand had reached down and taught it the trick. People posted videos of trees leaning all in one direction, then in the other, like congregations swaying to a hymn. Somewhere east, a ring road took a direct hit from something low and rotating; cars skated in place like fish under ice and then slid. The headline said TORNADO; the footage looked like a new animal unclassified, wind with a spine.

Farmers watched their orchards drown in rain from skies that had not held a drop the week before. A man who had built greenhouses with his brother and his brother's brother stood in their wreckage and said nothing for a full minute before deciding on a joke he could live with: "We should have bolted them down to the planet." The laugh he made after did not contain a laugh.

The Engineer, walking the crest, felt the reservoir breathing against the wall—a slow pressure you could almost sync your lungs to if you were willing to belong to it. Fog coiled around the intake structures like tame smoke. At the parapet, her handheld showed humidity in numbers she had only previously seen in jungle reports. She stared at the sky's new behavior and thought about how they'd modeled surface fluxes and thermal plumes and called the outliers conservative when they didn't fit. She chose the word weather as the bucket to hold her unease because weather is allowed to misbehave without anyone resigning.

The Scientist's instruments began to teach her the weather without glass. Aerosol counts climbed; upper-air

                    Susan Trott

soundings described temperature inversions stacked like bad pancakes. The lake's diurnal breath—cool by night, hot by day—coupled with the basin in a feedback that made the atmosphere sit and spin. A colleague sent her a clip of a storm forming over a salt flat in Bolivia and asked, *Does this look familiar?* She typed back, *It looks like our lake has hired the sky as a consultant.*

In town, the bakery learned to bake at dawn because afternoon ovens steamed. Flour clumped. Bread stuck. The baker took to propping the door with two bags now and swearing with a creativity that started to earn her a small following. She wrote HUMIDITY IS THEFT on a chalkboard and sold out of everything by ten.

By then the lake had begun to boil in places—not a rolling boil, not white, not anything that would make you step back fast at a stovetop, but an insistence of bubbles that arrived without ripples to announce them. They slid up from nowhere, silver coins minted in silence. Boys in shorts poked them with sticks and laughed at the way the water made a noise like a swallowed secret. Fishermen avoided those places without comparing notes.

Susan Trott

V. The Rift

The day the rift arrived, no one saw a line open from horizon to horizon. It was not theatrics. It was a negotiation decided offstage and delivered by courier. The quake that came with it did not snap houses from their foundations or knock stalactites from cavern ceilings in heroic footage. It pressed. It lengthened. It asked the continent to be a different shape and the continent obliged, the way a body shifts to make room for a new breath.

People felt it in their teeth. In a machine shop, a stack of feeler gauges slid, chink chink chink, as if counting. In a high school, a row of lockers rippled so slightly you would have sworn you were dizzy if everyone else hadn't stopped and lifted their chins like hounds. In the gallery under the dam, the Engineer watched the drip rate on six drains climb in unison like a choir. She said "Okay," out loud to no one, and the steadied rates said "Okay" back in a cadence that did not reassure.

Up on the surface, a field that used to be a rectangle forgot an angle and became a trapezoid. Fenceposts listed like sailors after a wake. A ridge out west grew a shadow it had not budded before, a crease like the beginning of a thought. The Scientist's map, up on the trailer wall, finally stopped pretending to be a riddle and became a picture anyone could read: ribs, spokes, all drawing toward an absence that was growing—an area that had graduated from being dense rock to being a problem.

She widened her search window and watched the little dots realign. They were not doing what reservoir quakes do when they relax a shore. They were doing what ice does when spring requires honesty. She sent her boss a note that contained the words uncontrolled and basin-scale. He forwarded it to a list of people whose names had previously read like weather: Secretaries, Directors, Commissioners. Replies came back with the brand new urgency of men who had just heard a word in their own language after a week in a foreign country.

At the shoreline, the Villager brought his stick and his granddaughter and found the top knife mark dry by a span he could not explain with evaporation or wind. He did not perform the math; he stood the stick where it had been and told the girl a story about springs waking up deep below and finding new ways to tell the surface what to do. She wanted an answer with numbers. He gave her a story because stories can be wrong and still be useful.

The dam held and looked good doing it. Its face stayed clean. The hairlines in the spillway apron went from meaningful to more meaningful. The Engineer's deputy printed reports in green that said the same sentence in four fonts. She went down to the lowest place the public was allowed and then stepped past the sign and went

     Susan Trott

lower. The walls sweated an intimacy that made her feel like a trespasser in the body of something alive. When she put her hand out this time, there was no pretense: a note, long and even, moving through stone like a spoke moves through wheel. The word she had refused took itself out of her pocket and put itself in her mouth: rift.

The quake that followed refused to behave with an epicenter. Instruments drew it as a wave with the scale of a country. Glasses shook in cupboards hundreds of miles apart with the same petty rhythm. Apartment elevators stopped at floors and waited. Helicopters vectored home without being asked. The Villager felt it come up through his feet and into his knees and spine and skull; it held him by the back of the neck and said, *You live on something that can change its mind.*

In cities far away, the news used graphics to explain what a rift is and what a rift is not. They put the dam in a corner box and moved lasers along red lines on a digital map that did not register the sound. The Scientist muted them and listened. The tremors had been rehearsals; this was the overture. She printed one more map and this time, around the absence, she did not draw a neat circle. She drew an ugly, honest shape and wrote in the margin, *No center. Only preference.*

By night the rift announced itself to eyes. Along a low ridge, the ground tore in a line the length of a small town's main street. It was not a canyon yet. It was a wound that had decided to stop being modest. In the morning people

came to stand by it with coffee and dismay. They took
pictures. Someone threw a rock in and waited to hear it
land and did not, not because it was deep, but because the
ground was still talking louder. The sound made it
impossible to believe in falling.

Susan Trott

———

Susan Trott

VI. The Vanishing Lake

The water retreated like a mood. At first the decline lived in decimals the Engineer could hide in a paragraph: heat, wind, a new regime of fetch. She wrote the numbers in her notebook and did not place her pencil where it could see her hand shake. The Villager's stick said otherwise. The lake licked lower, left a wet ring that dried into a belt, left that ring below another ring and another, a set of lives taken off a tree.

The marina learned a new verb: strand. Outboard motors leaned into the air like fish trying to remember a different time. Pilings showed their creosote to the sun and looked suddenly embarrassed. On the north shore, a slope of drowned cottonwoods reappeared as a fringe of antlers on a deer's skull: bleak, elegant, accusatory.

Engineers blamed surface losses. Hydrologists blamed a subsurface outflow through formations they hadn't modeled hard enough. The press releases used words like pathway and exchange. The Scientist stood on the parapet and watched oily sheens form where the bubbles came, watched steam vent from seams as if the lake had learned to exhale in cursive. She put a hand over her own mouth and did not know she'd done it until she felt her breath warm her knuckles.

The first sinkhole appeared in a cove where teenagers liked to drink and tell each other the kinds of secrets that keep you alive into your twenties. It opened with no drama—no swirl, no scream, just a sigh—and the water slipped into it like a focused thought. The hole made a sound that everyone present would describe differently later, as if the brain had to invent a word to endure it. One boy said it sounded like a throat clearing in a cathedral. A girl said it sounded like a door latching on a room that had always been there.

Over the next day three more mouths appeared—dark, perfectly undecorated, refusing to foam. People gathered and took videos until a deputy with a voice that could make dogs sit asked them not to. The recordings that got out were viewed by millions, muted by most. The view counter ticked like a Geiger counter in a movie. Comments arrived with the same old appetite for being right in public. Nobody's sentence dented the holes.

By afternoon, the drop could be measured without tools. Docks sat on mud like stranded centipedes. A boat ramp that had once been modestly useful became an absurd stairway into air. Fish congregated in thick, panicked knots in bays whose backs were being turned into shelves. The wildlife service came with nets and buckets and not enough time.

Steam learned boldness. It did not whisper up anymore; it spoke. Thin spires rose from mottled patches like the first candles in a church that intends many more. The air above

                    Susan Trott

the lake turned into a lens you could see. On the parapet, visitors pressed their forearms to the rail and felt their hair curl. Photographers worked in fog-proof housings and swore under their breath when lenses filmed nothing but milk.

The Engineer called for drawdown to ease pressure on the abutments; the control room answered with a list of other calls and the same problem in all of them: where to send it. Downstream had already learned the new weather and had made its own arguments. She cut all the water she could cut without lying and stood in the gallery again, listening to a drip that now came sometimes as a hiss.

Elsewhere, at a private airstrip, a pilot climbed through three thousand feet of cloud that smelled like warm stone and found the top as flat as a table. He banked and saw a field of anvils shading the valley. He radioed a friend: *It's making its own storms.* The friend said, *That sentence shouldn't exist,* and the pilot said, *Neither should this picture.* He sent the Scientist the image later that night. She looked at the little thumbprint of the dam on the edge of an atmosphere it had commissioned and finally said her first clear prayer in years, addressed to nothing in particular: *Let them listen before the listening is only for memory.*

The next morning, the lake's loss went from centimeters to hands. People who had lived on coasts felt the old gut feeling of a tide going wrong—water pulling too hard, too long—except inland has no tide table, no moon to blame, no dependable return. News anchors began to speak in passive voice as if the grammar could soften the physics. "Water levels are being observed to decline." "Steam plumes are understood to be increasing." "The situation is being monitored."

The Villager took his granddaughter down to the place where his grandmother's hill had become a bay and then a shallow and now a mudflat and showed her the blackened stumps that were once orchard. In the air above them floated a taste like iron filings and rain. He told her to listen. She said, "To what?" He said, "To what you cannot hear yet." She stood very still and did.

In the control room, someone proposed a ceremony to reassure the public—a ribbon of relief, a speech about stabilization, a gathering on the crest to thank the teams for their work during a challenging period. The suggestion slid through email like a fish in a current. People signed off with their initials, which were many and confident. The Engineer saw the calendar invitation appear and accepted it with a blank face she had practiced for meetings where numbers were more polite than men. The Scientist closed the invite and opened the drain data and spoke her first adjective out loud to the empty trailer. "Accelerating," she said, and the word stayed in the air as if it had mass.

By evening, the lake had taken on the expression of a person about to say something they know will be regretted. The wind died. The steam stood straight. Birds

     Susan Trott

left. A sheet of water, a whole long reach of it, lowered itself as if a hand had been withdrawn from underneath.

On the shore, the Villager knelt and pressed his palm to mud where yesterday there had been a wave. Heat came up into his bones. He turned to tell his granddaughter to get into the truck and discovered he had no voice that could travel the distance between his mouth and her ears. He waved. She ran and laughed because running is a joke you tell the air. When she reached him he put his hand on her hair and held it there, felt her heat, catalogued it as if listing could protect.

The ceremony for the next morning remained on the calendar. The drones were charged. The ribbon had been ordered in a blue chosen to reassure. The speeches were being polished to a shine you could see your face in. On a desk someone had placed a pair of gold scissors that could cut anything except what was coming.

     Susan Trott

VII. Cataclysm

Morning came in on felt feet. The sky wore a clean shirt. The wind, for once, stayed home. Someone had polished the podium to a mirror; you could see the lake in it, pretending stillness.

Drones rose and found their marks. The ribbon—calming blue—pulled lightly in a courteous breeze. The dignitaries practiced their smiles. The band waited for a downbeat that would never come.

The Engineer stood at the parapet with her notebook and a grief she could not yet name. The Scientist, two railings down, held a tablet that refused to lie for her anymore. The Villager parked his truck half a mile from the crest and lifted his granddaughter onto the hood because that made her taller and therefore, he thought, safer. The air smelled like a stone in the rain.

A tremor arrived with the tact of a cough in a church. People looked for the person who had coughed. The tremor left, courteous to a fault.

Then the lake's face made a decision.

It started as a soft, circular failure—the way a bedsheet settles when a person stands up—then tightened as if a hand had reached down and pinched. A whirl formed, too neat to be natural, and too large to be anything else. It took a moment for the eye to accept the scale: the circle's rim now reached from shore to shore. The surface lowered inside that rim as if someone were pulling the plug on a planet.

On the PA, someone said, "Please remain calm," and the microphone dutifully amplified the lie.

The whirl dug in. Its throat darkened. Water that had always pretended to be forever revealed itself as a number. Shorelines advanced as if brave. The marina's boats spun once, twice, and lay down in slow disbelief. A forest of drowned cottonwoods exhaled and showed their black antlers. The ribbon on the platform lifted and leaned toward the throat as if to offer itself.

Steam rose in thin pencils from a hundred seams, then from a thousand, then from everywhere the whirl's geometry said yes. The pencils thickened to columns. Sound found them: a million kettles turned high. The air turned to glass and shook.

"Down!" the Engineer shouted, because there is always at least one instruction that makes sense. The Scientist did not duck. She filmed. The Villager put his hand on the back of his granddaughter's neck and kept it there to remind himself exactly where she was in the world.

          Susan Trott

The throat opened.

Water went to it with the eagerness of gravity. The surface dropped in long, accelerating breaths. The lake spoke a note no instrument could hold. Shore mud blistered. Steam erupted not from above but from within, each plume punching a hole through itself.

The first explosion came late, which made it worse. The world had time to imagine mercy. Then the seam below found a pocket of heat, and the two oldest things—fire and water—met without supervision.

It was not a bang. It was a lift. The ground came up under everyone, under everything, as if a giant had stood beneath and shouldered the world. The wall rose and settled in one slow motion that broke glass in a radius you could measure in counties. The band's cymbals toppled and walked. The blue ribbon snapped without help from scissors and blew away like a stroke of paint.

The second explosion learned from the first. It turned the place where the whirl had been into a throat that would not close. Water became steam faster than language, and the steam took stone with it—magma quenched to glass and shattered, country rock flayed into grit, a century of geologic patience aerosolized and taught to fly. The column went up so fast the eye thought it was still until you noticed the birds caught in it had no time to disagree.

Shock arrived as a pressure that found your organs and squeezed. The air discovered edges and used them. A sheet of sound rolled across the basin and kept going until the mountains turned it into a long, shameful echo. Drones failed all at once and fell like a flock remembering gravity. The Engineer saw the first row of dignitaries crumple without knowing where the force had come from; she pulled a technician behind the parapet and felt concrete hum like a struck bell. The Scientist's tablet left her hands and went over; she didn't follow it by one decision.

Steam learned how to be storm. Lightning stitched the column from within, a rush of white nerves. The sky turned the wrong color, a bruised yellow that made the living look unripe. Ash began to fall, warm as breath. People put hands to heads for no reason except that the world felt like it could come off.

The throat widened. The lake emptied like a conviction abandoned. New mouths opened around the first—ring faults, the Scientist would have named them later if there had been a later—each one a lip that sank and allowed more water to become more steam to make more room for more sinking. The ground tore in quiet where the roar drowned it, new cracks paying out in white lines like the fast hatching of a crazed artist.

The Villager lifted the child and ran without style. The road had not been built to hold a morning like this. It tried. It failed politely—corners slumped, shoulders gave way, a slope advertised itself as a trap and then was. He put the truck into low and asked it to be a boat; it was not a boat.

     Susan Trott

He stopped, gathered the girl, and went up a hill that had always looked like a joke and now acted like a friend.

On the crest, the Engineer smelled hot metal and knew without looking which bearing had seized below her and why it didn't matter. She yelled names that were also commands. She knew the evacuation routes; they were poems she'd written during planning and never wanted to recite. The stairwell filled with breath and footsteps and the hot chalk smell of panic. The concrete under her boots ran a new vibration up her bones, a steady, endless thunder—not discrete quakes, not a series of insults, but the sound of tearing that had decided not to stop.

The Scientist crawled to the rail and made the mistake of looking directly into the column. Her eyes offered her metaphors like nervous jokes: a tree, a sword, a city, a birth. None of them honored it. She understood, finally, what her maps had been trying to say: *No center. Only preference.* The basin had not chosen a point. It had chosen a way of being.

The column reached for altitudes pilots use for their private faith. It punched the tropopause like wet paper and went on. The upper winds, insulted, tried to carry it and failed. In homes hundreds of miles away windows went white. In kitchens plates migrated. In a field a horse lay down and put its head on the ground because animals sometimes remember the instructions we forgot.

Then the lateral blast came—the thing steam does when it finds a wall and prefers not to go up anymore. It came low and fast, dense with water and knives of glass, hotter than stories. It hit the dam's flanks and leapt, hit the valley and scoured, hit the visitor center and did not leave a shape anyone would later agree had been a building. The bandstand went in a white breath. The podium's mirror turned to sand and then to air.

The Engineer and those who had followed her into a lower gallery felt the pressure wave go over like a hand pressed to a blanket. Their ears rang. Their mouths tasted pennies. The emergency lights flickered and reconsidered and decided to work. Concrete dust turned the flashlight beams into ropes.

Above ground, the lake was no longer a lake. It was a throat and a ring and, in the near reaches, a floor of mud that could not remember being anything else, now scored by boiling seams. The air lay on everything like a wet weight. The sky shuddered with continuous lightning. Ash fell in flour that stuck to sweat. A plane far above turned and ran and did not clear anything in time to avoid learning fear it would never unlearn.

When the main release paused—because even catastrophe must breathe—the silence that followed had a shape. You could hear things you never get to hear: boulders rolling as if they were thoughts, trees trying to stand up in soil that had decided to be soup, the faraway high shriek of steel losing an argument with geometry.

Susan Trott

And then the second breath began.

This one lasted longer. It found deeper seams. It made a sound that, to those who would survive long enough to speak of it, could only be described by negatives: not thunder, not wind, not train, not god. The rift opened from the throat outward with the efficiency of a zipper and the ugliness of a wound. When it stopped, it stopped not because mercy had arrived but because gravity had found a new place to rest.

Where the lake had been, there was a mile of air and then red. The new chasm stood rimmed in fuming glass and raw stone. The column now fed from a place no one had intended to put on a map. Ash bands circled. The sun, when it found them, turned into a coin minted wrong.

People ran until running was over. Some lived because they were lucky and some because luck mispronounced their names. The Villager and the child lay in a ditch that had learned to be useful. The Scientist found the Engineer by the feeling of a hand in dust reaching for a shoulder and choosing it. They looked at each other with the look of colleagues who have become family without agreeing and did not say anything because there was nothing to say that would not make it smaller.

Susan Trott

VIII. Aftermath

It rained black for three days. Not constantly—nothing that dramatic—just in fits that turned noon to evening and left gutters full of paste. Water in sinks came out brown and then did not come out. Radios talked in halves of sentences. Someone said the word curfew and meant kindness by it. The sky's color became a habit.

The ash tasted of metal and teeth. Cars learned to draw in lungs of their own and died coughing. Fields played at being beaches and lost. The inland hurricanes—your made-up storms—found a cause in the new heat engine and took it personally. A band of rain walked across a desert that had been allergic to rain and left it drowning. A tornado inspected a mountain town with the attentiveness of an auditor and left a ledger of splinters.

Maps were updated in pencil because ink felt presumptuous. Where a lake had been, cartographers left gray and a hatch and a word: Rift. The scale bar had to learn humility. Pilots flew the long way around or did not fly. Satellites saw a plume long as a continent and voted to watch, because there was nothing else to vote for.

The Engineer walked the galleries with a flashlight her hand had learned without asking. The dam stood. That was both miracle and joke. It had been built to hold back a lake that no longer existed. It felt like a cathedral after an excommunication.

The Scientist wrote notes no one would read soon. Phreatomagmatic column to ~40–50 km. SO estimates large enough to do years' worth of sky work. Ring-fault collapse ongoing. She wrote the sentences because writing sentences is a way to survive the hours between disasters and because later someone would need words that did not panic when read out loud.

The Villager took his granddaughter to the hill that had saved them and showed her how the horizon had moved. He told her the names of the trees because names are a kind of shelter. He did not tell her whether their house still existed, because he didn't know, and because he suspected the answer was now so complicated that yes and no were not opposites anymore.

Weeks learned to count differently. Sunrises arrived late, pink through milk. The temperature forgot its arithmetic. A harvest failed with a dignity that made farmers set their hats on fenceposts and leave them. Rivers downstream ran wrong—first low, then high with rain no one upstream had reported. Fish died in the new heat and in the new cold, both. Birds migrated without maps and found places that were not the places they had been told were places. People in cities far away woke with the sensation of a pressure above their faces and did not have a word for it in their language.

Susan Trott

Messages circulated with the small, stubborn courier of human kindness. Do you have batteries? I have water. Can you watch my mother's dog? Are you safe? A photograph made the rounds: two hawks perched on the bent arm of a crane, looking unimpressed. Under it someone wrote, They stayed.

On the first clear night the stars came back in a different order. Not actually, but that's how it felt. The column had thinned to a smear. The rift glowed in places and breathed in others. Airplanes came like thoughts and turned away like regrets. Somewhere far to the east a city saw a sunset the color of old coins and posted it with a caption that did not mention the cause. People liked the photo because it was beautiful and liking is one of the small levers left to us.

The Engineer stood with the Scientist on the parapet that no longer had a job and watched a heat-haze argue with a cold layer and lose. "We should name it," the Engineer said, because naming is a way to stop looking away. The Scientist shook her head. "It already has a name," she said. "It's the Earth."

They did not put a plaque on the wall. There would be time for plaques later, after the dust learned again how to fall in private and the taste of metal left milk. For now there were lists and boots and hands. For now the dam, absurd and proud, kept standing as if to apologize for a thing it had not done but had undeniably invited.

The Villager sat on the hill with the child and taught her how to listen to a planet that had stopped whispering. He said, "Once, people made a lake because they needed to believe the future could be held still. It worked, for a little while." She said, "And then?" He looked at the wound that had become a horizon and at the sky that had learned a new shade of dark. "And then the Earth reminded us what moving means."

In time, a new sea would take that place, thick with birth and warm like an old argument. In time, people would tell the story and be wrong about the details but right about the lesson. In time, ash would be soil and soil would be food and food would be kindness again. In time, some child would stand on a different parapet and throw a stone and listen for the splash and find that it spoke.

For the people who were there, time would divide cleanly: before the morning the lake fell, and after.

We thought we had dammed the river. Instead, we had damned the Earth.

Susan Trott

ACKNOWLEDGMENTS

My thanks to those who build, and to those who listen.

To the engineers, scientists, and dreamers who balance vision with humility, and to every voice that warns when the ground begins to shift.

To Jim, who steadies the current.

And to readers who stand on the parapet with me — thank you for hearing the quiet between the words.

Thank you.